HAUNTED HOUSE
TALES

retold by
Corinne Denan

illustrated by
Ann Toulmin-Rothe

Troll Associates

Haunted House Tales: Upside-Down Ghost, Naden; *Strange House*, Cram.

Copyright © 1980 by Troll Associates, Mahwah, N.J.

Library of Congress# 79-66335
ISBN 0-89375-336-X/0-89375-335-1 (pb)

CONTENTS

The Thing at the Foot of the Bed

Once there was a boy named Bert. Bert was cheerful and friendly. He had a lot of friends, and people liked him. Most of the time. Every once in a while, though, Bert's friends wished he were someplace else. That was because Bert talked a lot. In fact, he talked an *awful* lot.

Bert talked about anything and everything. If someone brought up a subject, Bert knew all about it. If he didn't know all about it, he certainly had an opinion. Sometimes Bert's opinions were wrong. Once in a while they were right. But right or wrong, Bert always sounded very sure of himself. And he was. No one could tell Bert *anything*.

But there was one time when even Bert had to admit that he talked too much.

It all started at a party one night before Halloween. Bert and his friends were having a good time telling scary stories, because Halloween is the best time for that. Bert, of course, was telling most of the stories—as usual.

The stories were all about witches and wizards

and goblins and ghosts. Halloween is the best time for them, too.

"Well, I don't mind telling such stories, or hearing them," said Bert. "But it's all non-sense—that's for sure."

"You mean you don't believe in witches and wizards and goblins and ghosts?" asked one of Bert's friends.

Bert really laughed about that. "No, I don't," he said. "In fact, I don't believe in anything I can't see. And I don't believe in anything that's not real."

"Then you wouldn't be *afraid* of a witch or a goblin?" asked one friend.

"Or a wizard or a ghost?" said another.

Bert glanced around with a smug look on his face. "That's right," he said. "I wouldn't be afraid at all. I'm not afraid of anything."

It was just about this time that some of Bert's friends began wishing once again that he were somewhere else. Then his friend Charlie said, "Okay, Bert, let's prove it."

Bert looked a little surprised. "Prove what?" he said.

"Let's prove that you're not afraid of anything."

"And just how are we going to do that?" Bert asked, his big smile showing how willing he was.

8

"Let's see if you dare to spend one night in the old Stapleton place. That's how we'll do it," said Charlie.

There was silence for a minute. Finally, someone said, "You mean that spooky old haunted house out on the edge of town?"

"That's the one. How about it, Bert?"

Bert didn't hesitate for even one second. Later, everyone had to admit that. He just smiled again, and, in his sure-of-himself voice, he said, "I'll do it for certain. There's no such thing as a haunted house, and there's no such thing as a ghost. And now I'll prove it."

It was decided then and there that Bert would spend the next night—Halloween—in the old Stapleton place. All his friends would walk to the haunted house with him. But they weren't going to hang around!

The next night Bert and his friends met in the center of town.

"Sure is a perfect night for a haunting," said one of them.

"Sure is," Bert agreed.

It was, indeed, a good night for haunting. The air was cool and crisp, the sky was dark and overcast. The moon and stars were covered with layers of thick, swirling clouds. A light rain

9

started to fall as the group began to walk to the edge of town. The wind whipped at their backs and sent dead leaves brushing past their ears.

"You sure you want to do this, Bert?" asked Charlie.

"Sure I do," Bert said, his smile as calm and steady as ever.

Brave as they all thought they were, not one of Bert's friends would walk beyond the gate of the old Stapleton place. But Bert didn't seem to be bothered at all. He just waved to everyone and pushed open the rusty old gate. Then he walked up the cracked and overgrown sidewalk.

The old Stapleton house stood alone on a hill. It was a strange house, haunted or not. It was three stories high, with steep, pointed gables. Its windows were long and narrow, with broken panes and drooping shutters.

The roof was sagging. The paint had long since peeled from the shingles. Loose shutters banged and creaked in the wind. Bert stood there on the sidewalk for a minute, looking up at the house. Then he tucked the blanket he was carrying up under his arm, and started toward the door.

"Hey, Bert, wait a minute! We forgot something," Charlie called. "Come back here."

11

Bert walked back to the gate. "What's up?" he asked.

"We thought maybe you should take this along, just to be on the safe side," said Charlie. And he handed Bert a small, black pistol.

"Oh, for Pete's sake," said Bert. "What do I want this for?"

"Just to be on the safe side," Charlie repeated. And all the others nodded.

Bert looked at them and laughed. Then he put the pistol in his pocket. "Okay, you scaredy-cats. I'll keep it with me if it makes you all feel better." Then he waved again and walked back to the house.

Bert's friends stood nervously by the gate until their friend pushed open the creaky front door and went inside. In a few moments they could see the wavering light of the candle he had brought with him.

"Guess there's no more we can do here," said Charlie.

"Yeah, we might as well go on home," said someone else.

And the small group moved off into the dark and windy night.

Inside, Bert walked through the gloomy old rooms. Cobwebs hung everywhere. The rotten

floorboards groaned with every step he took. The wind caught the shutters and banged them repeatedly against the house.

"Well, I know what those sounds are," Bert thought. "There's nothing mysterious here at all. If this is what they call a haunted house, I'll have the last laugh for sure."

Bert walked up the creaking old stairs and found a large bedroom. "I guess I might as well sleep in here," he said. He settled himself on the squeaky old bed. Soon he realized he was shivering from the cold. He pulled his warm, white blanket all the way up to his neck. Then he took the small pistol from his pocket and put it on the dusty table beside the bed.

The air was cold and musty. Bert lay there quietly, listening as the shutters banged, and rain whispered against the windows. From time to time Bert heard other noises—a slight rustling, a tap-tapping, a muffled thud. And each time he said to himself, "There's no such thing as ghosts, and that's that!"

Maybe Bert fell asleep. He never was quite sure about that. But he was sure that when he opened his eyes, the rain and wind had stopped. He could see the moonlight coming in through the broken shutters. Everything was still.

14

"Well, that's a whole lot better," Bert thought. Then he said out loud, "There won't be any ghosts walking around on a nice, clear, moonlit night like this. Besides, there's no such thing as ghosts."

All of a sudden, Bert held his breath. *There was something at the foot of the bed!* Two eyes, shining in the moonlight. Two eyes, just staring at him. The eyes never moved. Neither did Bert. He was too scared!

For a long, long time, Bert stayed very still. Not a muscle twitched. The eyes kept staring at Bert. Bert kept staring at the eyes. Then slowly—ever so slowly—Bert reached out toward the table beside him. His fingers curled around the handle of the small, black pistol.

"I don't know if you can shoot a ghost," he thought, "but I'm going to find out."

The eyes just kept staring, never moving.

"No ghost is going to get me," Bert thought. And slowly, slowly, he raised the pistol. He aimed it right at one of the ghostly staring eyes.

Bert held his breath. Then he pulled the trigger.

The eyes at the foot of the bed stopped staring!

Afterward, some of Bert's friends claimed they could hear the scream all the way into town. But

16

of course, that wasn't true. It was a mighty scream, though. Even Bert himself had to admit that later. You see, the scream was Bert's.

He had pulled his blanket up so high that his feet stuck out, and his toenails reflected the moonlight. And big, brave Bert had taken careful aim—and put a bullet in his own big toe.

Upside-Down Ghost

The house was haunted . . . *everybody* said so. That was the first thing Mary and Tod Garrett had heard when they moved to the small Vermont town.

"That house you're moving into is haunted for sure. Everybody knows that," said Mr. Taylor at the grocery store.

"Mind you. Strange things have happened up there. I'm just telling you for your own good," said Mrs. Hawkins, who ran the local gas station.

"You're new around here. Keep your eyes open," warned the Chief of Police. Then he added in a low voice, "I don't believe in all that, of course. But—well, I'm only telling you."

Mary and Tod just laughed. Hauntings and ghosts and such things were not part of their world. Mary wrote mystery stories, and she was very good at it. But her stories were full of *real* things. Nothing imaginary, like ghosts. And Tod was a lawyer. His world was full of real things, too—like judges and juries and evidence—and facts. And so they just laughed at the idea of ghosts in their house.

But their son Tim didn't laugh. He'd never actually seen a ghost—and he wasn't sure he wanted to. But he was perfectly willing to believe that there *might* be a ghost in the house.

"It *looks* like a ghost could live here," Tim told his parents.

Mary and Tod Garrett had to agree with that. The house was big and rambling. Its gray shingles were peeling here and there, and the shutters hadn't seen a paintbrush in years.

The outside of the house needed fixing, but the inside was just beautiful. Great dark beams crossed the ceilings, and the floors shone from the loving care they had received over the years. In the living room was a huge fireplace, its thick stones blackened by the smoke of countless logs.

"That's probably where the ghost hides out," said Tim, trying to look up the wide chimney.

"And I bet he'll come down every night to visit us—right?" said his father with a smile.

"No. Probably not every night, Dad," Tim said seriously. "But I'll bet he comes down on Halloween."

"In that case," observed his mother, "we have almost two months to wait."

In the next few weeks, the Garretts forgot about ghosts. There were new friends and a new

school for Tim. His mother had a mystery story to finish. His father started work in a new law office. And of course, they all had a great deal to do before the rambling old house would seem like home.

This big house in the country was nothing like the small apartment in the city. From the tall, narrow windows of the living room, they could look out across acres of trees—now all red and gold in the autumn sun.

"Do you suppose we'll be lonely in the winter?" Mary wondered. "It's so different from the city. And this house is really pretty far from town."

"We've got each other for company," said Tod.

"And we have the ghost," said Tim. That made his parents laugh.

By the end of October, the Vermont weather had turned cold and crispy. The leaves crunched under Tim's feet as he walked up the road from where the school bus had left him. The lights of the house looked warm and comforting in the dark, cloudy gray of the afternoon. As he looked up, Tim saw smoke curling from the chimney.

"Hey, neat—Mom has a fire going," he thought, as he ran up the driveway.

But when Tim walked inside, there was no fire

in the great fireplace. He found his mother in the small back room she had made into an office.

"I saw smoke coming from the chimney," he told her.

"Honey, you're imagining things. Why don't you get something to eat? I have a few more pages to finish."

Tim ran outside again and looked up at the chimney. There was no smoke. He shrugged his shoulders and went back into the house.

That night they did have a fire in the big fireplace. Tim lay on the floor doing his homework. Mary and Tod were reading. Suddenly, all three of them stopped what they were doing. For there, warming its hands in front of the fire, was a rather small, rather gray ghost.

No one said anything at first. Then Tim cried, "It's the ghost! It's really the ghost! I can't believe it!"

"Well, you *can* believe it all right," said the ghost. "And it's about time, too. I've been up that chimney for three years now."

Tim's mother and father were still sitting like statues. But Tim really wasn't all that surprised. "Why have you been up there so long?" he asked.

"Because I can only come down once a year, on

Halloween—and only then if there's a fire in the fireplace," the ghost said. "It's a nuisance, believe me. For the last three years either the weather's been too warm for a fire or nobody's been at home. So I've been stuck!"

Tim's mother finally found her voice. "I think I'm losing my mind," she said.

"No, you're not," said the ghost, who now sat down in front of the fire. "It's me all right. I don't know why things are as they are, but unless it's Halloween and unless there's a fire in this chimney, I'm frozen solid up there. Oh, I can do things, mind you. I can make things happen, if I want to. But I can't come down. It certainly gets lonely."

"Hey, this is really terrific. We'll be sure to have a fire every Halloween so you can come down," Tim said to the ghost.

"This is not at all terrific," said his mother. "This is crazy!"

"I don't know *what* it is," said Tim's father, who had at last found his voice. "Tim, will you ask the ghost a question?"

"Why don't you ask him, Dad?"

"Because I cannot convince myself that I am actually talking to a ghost, that's why," said Tim's father. "Now would you mind asking him what happens if the fire dies out?"

"I disappear," said the ghost.

Without a word, Tim's father got up and went to the kitchen. He returned with a bucket of water, which he started to throw on the fire.

"Don't do that!" the ghost cried. "I just have one night a year!"

"Aw, please, Dad," Tim begged. "He's not hurting anything."

But Tim's father kept throwing water on the fire.

The ghost began to get smaller and smaller. Finally, he started to move up the chimney. But before he disappeared, they heard him say in a small voice, "You'll be sorry about this. I can make things happen, I told you. You'll see."

By the next morning Tim's mother and father were convinced that they had imagined the whole thing. "All this talk about ghosts," they said.

But Tim knew better. It had been a real ghost, all right. He kept thinking about what the ghost had said just before he disappeared.

Everything went on as usual for the next few days. But about a week after Halloween, the Garrett's world started to turn upside-down.

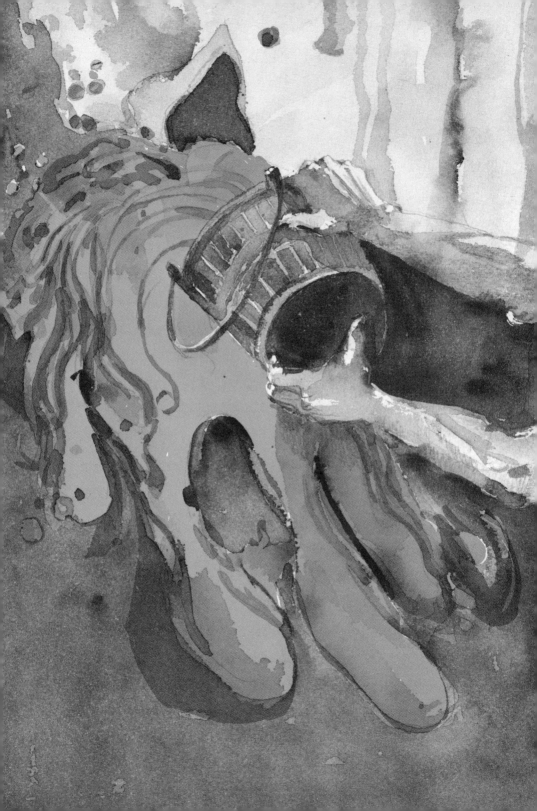

It was little things at first. Tim's mother got dressed one morning and looked at herself in the full-length mirror. Then she looked again. She seemed to be standing on her head. Tim's father turned on the shower, and water shot out all over the ceiling. When Tim ran downstairs for breakfast, he found himself back up in his room. The stairs were somehow going the wrong way.

The Garretts soon found out that the only way to get upstairs or downstairs was to walk backwards. It got on everyone's nerves. If they forgot to turn around before walking upstairs, sure enough—they'd land in the basement. One sleepy morning, Tim forgot so many times that he missed the school bus.

"I wish I could explain what's going on here," Tim's father grumbled.

"It's the ghost," Tim said. "I knew it."

"It is *not* the ghost," his mother said. "There is no such thing as a ghost."

"Then what did we all see? And what's doing all this?" Tim asked.

Nobody could answer him.

Things got even more hectic later on. When Tim's father tried to back the car out of the garage, he drove straight ahead through the wall!

And whenever Tim's mother turned on the lamp over her desk, the whole house went dark.

It wasn't that anything really terrible ever happened—except for the garage wall, of course. But it was all very annoying. Doors opened the wrong way. Hot water ran out of the cold water tap. Ice cubes melted in the freezer. Eggs froze in the frying pan. The carpet was up on the ceiling.

Milk poured up instead of down. The basement was up in the attic, and the attic was down in the basement. The dining room table turned upside-down. Mice began to chase the cat. The clock ticked backwards.

"We must all be going crazy!" said Tim's mother.

"It's the ghost. He *told* us we'd be sorry," said Tim.

His parents just looked at him. Then they looked at each other.

"Do you suppose it *could* be the ghost?" asked Tim's father.

"There is no such thing as a ghost, remember?" said Tim's mother. But she didn't sound as sure as usual.

The last straw was the Christmas tree. Tim and

his parents had spent a long time finding just the right tree. And they'd spent a long time decorating it for their first Vermont country Christmas. They put brightly colored packages under the tree. Then they went out to dinner.

When they came home and walked into the living room, they couldn't believe their eyes. The Christmas tree was upside-down! The ornaments and the tinsel were hanging straight up. And all around the bottom of the tree—which was now on the ceiling—were all the gaily wrapped packages.

"We're moving," said Tim's mother.

"As soon as possible," said Tim's father.

"I'm *telling* you, it's the ghost!" said Tim.

It took a while for the Garretts to find anyone who wanted to buy the house. Probably because everybody in the area had heard about the upside-down ghost. But at last they found a city family that wanted to try country living.

"We're moving back to the city," said Tod and Mary Garrett. "The world seems more right-side-up there."

The people who were buying the house looked at them a little strangely.

"I suppose you've heard about the ghost?"

Tim's father asked, pretending he was amused about it all.

"Oh, yes," said the man. "That's all anybody in town seems to talk about. But of course, we don't believe in ghosts!"

"Well, I've got to be honest with you," Tim's father said. And he told them the whole story.

The family just laughed. "When you come from the big city, you don't believe in ghosts," they said.

Tim and his mother and father looked at each other. But they didn't say anything more.

The Strange House

Ted spent only one night in that house. And it was very long ago. But never has he been able to forget the dark and terrible horror he experienced there. It will live with him forever.

This is what he remembers . . .

When school ended, Ted decided to visit his old friend, Mark Adams. The day he arrived, the two young men talked at lunch.

"I own a house here on Prince Street," Mark told him. "An elderly aunt of mine died last spring and left it to me."

"Do you live there by yourself?" Ted asked.

"Oh, no," Mark said. "I don't live there at all! The place is haunted."

Ted laughed. "Haunted? You're kidding!"

"Well, that's what they say," Mark told him seriously. "Let me tell you about it. I didn't know my aunt very well. In fact, no one was more surprised than I when she left me the house. Some people said she was a witch. All I know is that she was very strange.

"She had a friend who supposedly practiced black magic," Mark continued. "His name was Dr. Sar. When my aunt died, Dr. Sar thought that he was going to inherit her property. But, for some reason, she left it to me."

"What happened to Dr. Sar?" asked Ted.

"Well, according to gossip, he put a curse on the house and was never heard from again."

"I really can't believe all this," Ted said with a smile. "And if I know you, you don't either."

"All I know is that no one will live there," Mark told him. "I can't rent it or sell it. Everyone says it's haunted. No one ever sees or hears anything there, but they say it's haunted all the same."

"Why don't you live there yourself?" Ted asked.

"I've been thinking about it," Mark said. "It's silly to have it stand empty. In fact, two friends of mine have promised to spend Friday night with me in the house, just to see if it's haunted. Say," he said excitedly, "why don't you come along with us?"

"It might be fun at that," said Ted. "And if you can show me a real, live ghost, all the better!"

They both laughed and promised to meet on Friday.

That Friday evening after dinner, Ted joined Mark and his two friends—Richard and Frank. They all piled into Mark's tiny car and headed for the house on Prince Street. On the way, Mark told Ted more about the strange haunted house.

"My aunt lived there with an old servant woman," Mark said. "No one was ever seen going into the house. Except for Dr. Sar. People saw him go *in* the house lots of times. But no one ever saw him come *out*. Not once. In fact, one time some of the neighbors decided to set up a watch to see him leave. But he didn't leave. Yet the next day, they saw him walking up to the front door again!"

"Maybe there's a hidden back door," suggested Ted.

"No," said Mark with a shake of his head. "The house is kind of strange. The only doorway is in front. The house is attached to other houses on either side. In the back is a little courtyard. But that's surrounded by houses, too. There's no way out from there."

"Well, that is sort of strange," said Ted. He was beginning to feel just a little uneasy about the thought of spending a night in such a place.

"What's even stranger," Mark said, "is that once every year a group of people would suddenly arrive at the house. All night long there would be the sound of strange music and chant-

ing voices. The next morning, everyone would be gone. And they wouldn't come back again for another year."

Ted said nothing, but an uneasy feeling came over him again. "Oh, this is silly," he told himself. "There's no such thing as a haunted house. And besides, there are *four* of us!"

It was dark by the time they reached the house on Prince Street. It was in an old, neglected part of the city. The streets were narrow and crooked. Paper and trash fluttered in the breeze. There was a pale glow from a street light.

"Not exactly a cheerful spot," joked Frank.

Mark opened the huge, dark front door with his key. They walked inside. "The electricity isn't hooked up," he said, "but there are lanterns here."

They lighted the lanterns and looked around. The hallway was dusty and covered with cobwebs. Slowly, without speaking, the four young people walked through the rooms of the first floor. The rooms were still and nearly empty.

"This certainly doesn't look very haunted to me," said Richard. And all four of them began to feel better.

"Let's go upstairs," Mark said. "That's supposed to be the part that's haunted anyway. It's where my aunt probably held her yearly parties. Just wait until you see this."

They walked up the winding staircase and pushed open a door on the second floor. As they looked about, Mark's guests nearly dropped their lanterns.

"Didn't I tell you it was strange?" Mark asked with a shaky laugh.

The room was long, stretching all the way to the back of the house. The walls and the ceiling were painted black. But the floor shone with a brilliant, bloodlike red. From the middle of the ceiling hung a great white object.

"What is it?" Ted asked in a whisper. "It looks like some kind of horrible monster egg."

"I don't know what it is," Mark said. "But I've never seen anything like it. Maybe this was where Dr. Sar practiced his magic!"

No one wanted to stay in the room. They went up to the third floor, where they would sleep. Four small rooms were lined up in a row. Each opened onto the long, narrow hall.

"Let's see," said Mark, "I'll take the first room; Richard, the second; Frank, the third; and Ted, you take the last one. And even though no one believes in ghosts, let's all leave our lanterns burning and the doors open. If anyone hears anything at all or needs help, just yell and we'll all come running. Agreed?"

The other three nodded, and they all went to their rooms.

Ted was glad to see that the small room at the end looked almost normal. The walls were painted white, and the furniture, although dusty, was ordinary enough. He opened a window and set his lantern on the small bench in front of it.

There were no strange sounds. Ted began to relax a little. His eyes closed. Soon he was asleep.

Then, suddenly, his eyes snapped open. He was wide awake! The house was dark and still. His lantern had gone out. He could hear no sound from the other rooms. No sound anywhere. What had awakened him?

Ted realized that his legs felt numb. "That's it," he thought. "It's just cold in here. I'd better light the lantern again."

He rose from the bed and went over to the window. As he bent to pick up the lantern, his arm grew numb with cold. He felt the cold begin to creep throughout his body. Then he realized he could not move! He stood rooted to the spot, his legs like stone, his arms frozen at his sides.

The numbness crept higher. Now he could feel it at his throat.

He tried to scream, to call for help. But no words would come. He could make no sound at all!

"I'm turning to stone," he thought in terror. "My body is turning to stone. I can feel it happening. What is doing this to me?"

He did not know how long he stood there like a stone statue. But he could move nothing, not even his eyes. Only his mind seemed alive. He stared straight ahead at the open window, at the empty blackness before him.

Then, far away, he saw them. Two tiny, white lights in the distance. The lights grew larger and closer. He could not move. He could not get away. Then, framed in the open window, he could see that the lights were two pale, glaring eyes. They stared at him. He could only stare back, fear gripping his mind like needles of ice.

The eyes kept moving toward him. Closer and closer. What horror was this? Now the eyes were right in front of him, staring.

Then it happened. Like a great, oozing jellyfish, the eyes seemed to devour him. He could feel the cold, thick slime covering his body. And then it began to cover his head, his eyes, his mouth. It was drawing the life from him. He could not breathe. In terror, he finally gave himself up to this horrible death . . .

"Is he going to be all right?"

Slowly, Ted opened his eyes. He was lying on a small bed. Mark, Richard, and Frank stood nearby. A doctor was peering over him.

"What happened?" he cried. "Where am I?"

"It's all right now," Mark told him. "You're in the hospital. But you're all right."

Then his three friends told him what had happened.

Frank, whose room was next to Ted's, had not been able to sleep. So he called to Ted to see if he was still awake. After calling once or twice, he got out of bed and picked up his lantern. When he walked to Ted's door, he found it locked! He called the others, and they all tried the door. But it would not open.

Inside the room, they could hear footsteps and wild breathing. Then, they threw themselves against the door and broke it open.

There, in the middle of the room, lay Ted, quiet and lifeless. And the whole room—the floor, the walls, and the ceiling—was dripping with a thick, oozing slime.

Terrified, the three young men quickly dragged Ted from the room and fled from the house.

"But what was it?" Ted whispered. "What was it?"

No one could answer. No one was ever able to answer that question.

Later that night, the strange house on Prince Street burned to the ground. Not a timber was left standing, and the cause of the fire remained a mystery.

But no one—not Frank or Richard or Mark, and especially not Ted—could ever forget that one night in the house on Prince Street.